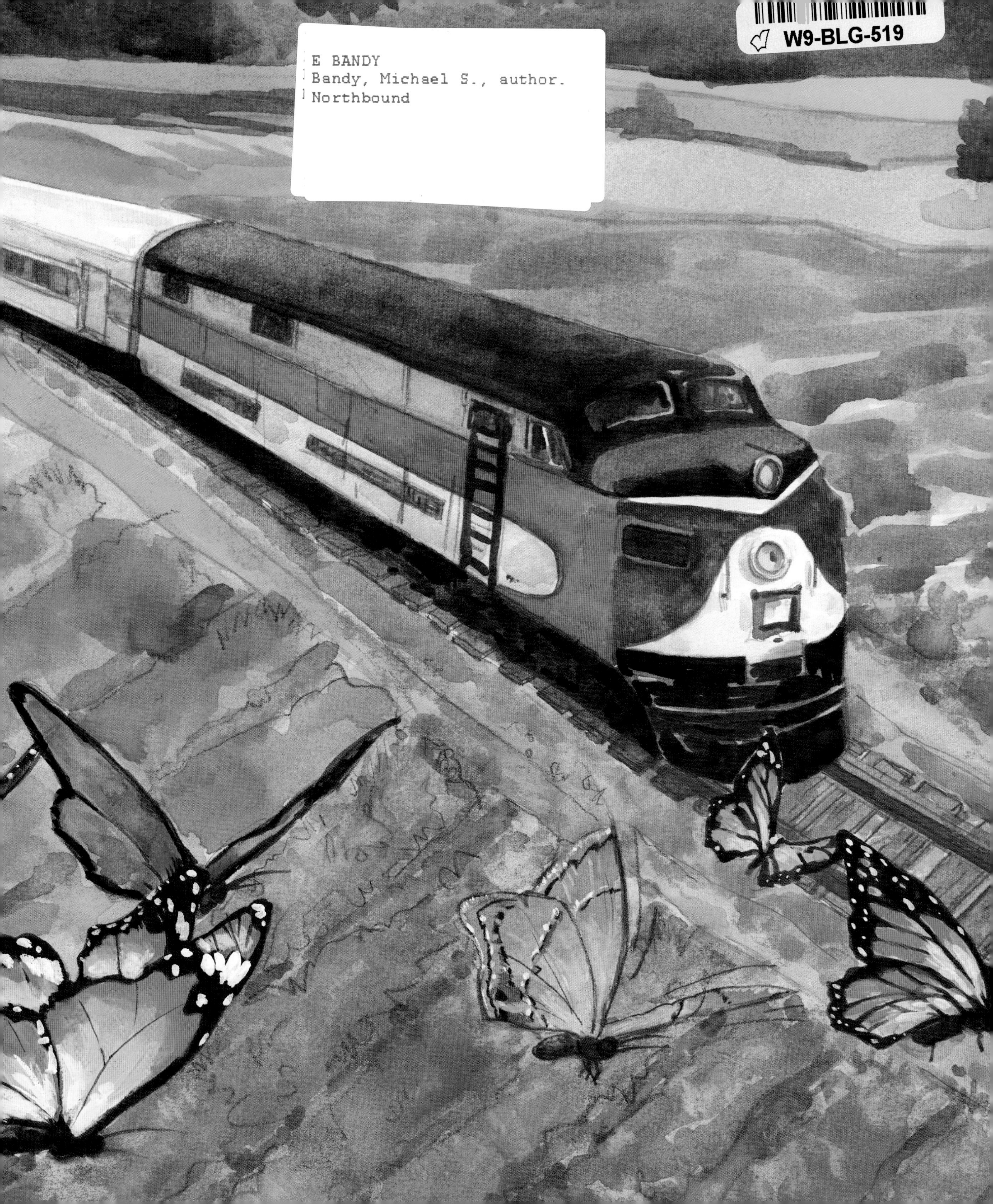

# NORTHBOUND

Michael S. Bandy and Eric Stein

illustrated by James E. Ransome

CANDLEWICK PRESS

**TRAINS!** The clickety-clack of the wheels and the low song of the whistles.

   As the huge engines rushed by our farm, Granddaddy and I always stopped our work to watch and to dream of climbing on board a powerful train and traveling to distant, strange places.

And then one day I got what I wanted the most.

Grandma was taking me for my first train ride! We were going north, all the way from Alabama to Ohio to visit my cousins.

The station was crowded with all sorts of people. The train was much bigger up close.

It was huge!

"All aboard!" the conductor shouted.

"All aboard!" I shouted back.

The conductor directed me and my grandma to the "colored only" train car.

Suddenly the train jerked forward.

The wheels squealed and squeaked as we slowly got under way.

*Woo, woo!* the whistle sounded.

"Woo, woo!" I shouted back.

The train moved faster and faster. I pressed my face up against the
window to get the best view.

At first we passed farms and little towns like ours.

Then we sped through tunnels. We practically flew over bridges.

Soon we were zooming by places that didn't look like anything I had ever seen before!

It was like I was seeing a movie, but it was real.

Now all I wanted was to explore the whole train. My grandma was so tired, she fell asleep. So I crept past her and started up the aisle.

The train swayed so much, I had to hold on to seats as I made my way to the front of the car.

Through the window, I saw the boy who had gotten on at our station.

But I was not allowed in his car.

"Next stop, Atlanta, Georgia," shouted the conductor as he trudged through our car, punching tickets.

Atlanta, Georgia! I had never seen so many different kinds of people all in the same place or such giant buildings. Even if I was only seeing them through the train window.

I was in heaven.

As we pulled out of the Atlanta station, the conductor came through and took the sign down from the door. I was so surprised.

It seemed as if I could go right through to the next car now. I guess Atlanta had some different rules from home.

COLORED ONLY
No Whites Allowed

Then the boy I'd seen before suddenly entered our car
and ran up to me.

"Hi, I'm Bobby Ray," he said.

"I'm Michael," I said.

"Do you want to explore?" Bobby Ray asked.

I looked at my grandma to see if it was okay.

She nodded and said, "Y'all be careful now."

"Yes, ma'am!" I shouted as Bobby Ray and I raced
to the next car.

Going from train car to train car while the train was moving was a little scary. It was loud, and the platform moved back and forth. It was kind of hard to keep your balance at first. But after a few times, it was easy for us.

We rushed straight through the cars full of folks sitting and
came upon a car with bunk beds stacked up behind curtains.
Amazing. People must sleep in those beds at night.

Then we came to a car that looked like the fanciest restaurant I had ever dreamed of. A waiter there told us he had worked on the trains his whole life. I guess he'd been just about everywhere!

This train was full of surprises.

When we got back to Bobby Ray's car, I was surprised to find lots of empty seats.

"Who's your new friend?" asked Bobby Ray's mom.

"Michael," Bobby Ray said.

"Go on, have a seat, Michael," she said.

I sat down, and Bobby Ray and I talked and talked.

Turns out Bobby Ray was just my age and even lived in the same town as me, though we'd never met before. That's probably because where we lived there were schools for people like Bobby Ray and different schools for people like me.

Bobby Ray really liked my collection of special green army men. I sure didn't let just anyone play with them, but Bobby Ray was my new friend.

Bobby Ray had lots of drawings of trains. He was a really good artist.

And we both had scars! Mine was on my elbow, from when I fell out of a tree. His was on his knee, from slipping on rocks by the creek.

"I'm making something for you," Bobby Ray said.

"What is it?" I asked.

"It's a surprise," Bobby Ray said. "You'll see."

But then the fun stopped. The conductor shouted, "Chattanooga, Tennessee, next stop."

Then he put the WHITES ONLY sign back up in Bobby Ray's train car. Bobby Ray handed me a rolled-up paper with a rubber band wrapped around it, but I didn't have time to look at it. The conductor whisked me down that aisle darn fast.

"That ain't fair, mister!" said Bobby Ray.

The conductor just grinned and looked back at him and kept moving me away.

Seemed like the rules on that train were always changing. It just didn't make any sense at all.

The next thing I knew, it was dark and Grandma was shaking me awake to see Cincinnati, Ohio! The train went over a long bridge. The glittery lights of the giant buildings looked like diamonds on the water below.

The signs between the cars had been taken down.

I didn't think I would ever experience anything as magical as that first train ride to Ohio.

But I was wrong. What I was about to see would stay with me forever.

In the drawing Bobby Ray gave me, I saw white folk sitting next to black folk in the same train car.

Of all the surprising new things I had seen on my journey, that was the most wonderful.

# AUTHORS' NOTE

**IN 1887, THE INTERSTATE COMMERCE ACT** was passed to regulate railroad rates and railcar commerce. But as it grew, its tentacles of regulation didn't stop there.

A myriad of legal cases were fought with respect to accommodations of travelers based on race: *Boynton v. Virginia*, *Plessy v. Ferguson*, and *NAACP v. St. Louis–Santa Fe Railway Company*, to name a few.

Some local jurisdictions said "separate but equal" was the appropriate way to address issues of race, while others forbade racial discrimination altogether. So how were these conflicting policies handled? In most cases, not very well.

Bus and rail companies would simply adjust to the policies of the local constabularies. Hence, movements such as Freedom Rides and sit-ins came about to combat Jim Crowism in public transportation.

In *Northbound: A Train Ride Out of Segregation*, Michael travels by train with his grandmother from Opelika, Alabama, to Cincinnati, Ohio, in the early 1960s. Growing up in the Deep South, Michael has become accustomed to racial indignities such as segregated schools, water fountains, and restaurants; they are his way of life. "That's just the way we do things down here" became his personal motto.

But this journey throws Michael for a loop. He doesn't know how to act, and he's not sure of his place. When he and his grandmother travel through one state, the colored signs go up. When they pass through another, the signs come down.

The only consistent thing in this trip is his newfound friendship with Bobby Ray. Whether they were traveling through the Tennessee Valley or the hills of Kentucky, their bond was life-changing.

---

### THANKS TO
Elizabeth Bicknell, Carter Hasegawa, Spencer Humphrey, Ed Labowitz, Karen Lotz, and Lisa Rudden

To my grandma Annie Bandy, for a train ride that changed my life.
My teacher Mrs. Callaway—"Read and read some more."
My mentor Sean Bailey—"Love what you write, write what you love."
MSB

For my mom, Sandy Stein
ES

To all of the young voices of the civil rights movement
who removed curtains between black and white cars everywhere
JER

---

Text copyright © 2020 by Michael S. Bandy and Eric Stein. Illustrations copyright © 2020 by James E. Ransome. All rights reserved. No part of this book may be reproduced, transmitted, or stored in an information retrieval system in any form or by any means, graphic, electronic, or mechanical, including photocopying, taping, and recording, without prior written permission from the publisher. First edition 2020. Library of Congress Catalog Card Number pending. ISBN 978-0-7636-9650-4. This book was typeset in Vollkorn. The illustrations were done in watercolor and collage. Candlewick Press, 99 Dover Street, Somerville, Massachusetts 02144. www.candlewick.com.
Printed in Shenzhen, Guangdong, China. 20 21 22 23 24 25 CCP 10 9 8 7 6 5 4 3 2 1